FOR DAVE MOUNFIELD

SPECIAL THANKS TO ZAC BROMILOW
FOR LETTING KEVIN POO ON HIS HEAD

OXFORD
UNIVERSITY PRESS

Great Clarendon Street, Oxford OX2 6DP
Oxford University Press is a department of the University of Oxford.
It furthers the University's objective of excellence in research, scholarship,
and education by publishing worldwide. Oxford is a registered trade mark
of Oxford University Press in the UK and in certain other countries

British Library Cataloguing in Publication Data

Data available

ISBN: 978-0-19-276614-4

1 3 5 7 9 10 8 6 4 2

Printed in China

Paper used in the production of this book is a natural,
recyclable product made from wood grown in sustainable forests.
The manufacturing process conforms to the environmental
regulations of the country of origin.

KEVIN

and the

BISCUIT BANDIT

BY THE REMARKABLE DOUBLE ACT THAT IS

PHILIP REEVE AND SARAH McINTYRE

OXFORD
UNIVERSITY PRESS

This is Kevin.

Kevin is a flying pony. But he's not just any old flying pony, oh no.

Roly-Poly Flying Ponies are the BEST sort of Flying Ponies.

Kevin lives in a town called Bumbleford. He has a big, raggedy nest on the roof of the tall building where his friends Max and Daisy live. Kevin's favourite things to do are:

- Flying around with Max and Daisy
- Eating biscuits

Kevin absolutely LOVES biscuits. His favourites are custard creams, but he also likes bourbons, pink wafers, chocolate chip cookies, chocolate digestives, jammie dodgers, and bonk-on-the-head biscuits. (Those are the chocolatey marshmallowy ones in the red and silver wrappers, you know the ones.)

Some people say that eating all those biscuits is what made Kevin so roly-poly, but Kevin doesn't mind. He thinks he is just the right shape for a flying pony.

ONE

THE BISCUIT BURGLARIES

It was midnight in Bumbleford. Max and Daisy were snoring in their beds, Kevin was snoozing in his nest on the roof, and even the ducks and swans and moorhens on the River Bumble were asleep, with their heads tucked under their wings. But those ducks and swans and moorhens were about to get a rude awakening because—

DANGANANGANANGANA

—the burglar alarm on the supermarket in Bumbleford High Street suddenly went off, splashing blue light across the shop fronts and filling the midnight air with noise.

Down on the river the swans and moorhens stuck their wings over their ears and grumbled about the racket, and a duck started writing a letter of complaint to the Town Council.

QUACK QUACK QUACK QUACK QUACK!

And just as they were starting to get used to the DANGANANGANANGANANG noise, it was joined by a second noise, a sort of WOO-WOO-WOO that grew louder and louder as the Bumbleford Police Force's fastest patrol car came racing into town to investigate.

The Bumbleford Police Force's fastest patrol car was also its only patrol car, and it wasn't even all that fast, because until very recently there hadn't really been much crime to fight in Bumbleford. In the past twenty years the Bumbleford Police Force had only dealt with one serious incident, and that was just somebody punching a dustbin. But now all that had changed! For seven nights in a row Bumbleford had been rocked by burglaries, and those beastly burglars were only interested in one thing—BISCUITS! The newsagent, the delicatessen, and all the cafés had been robbed, their shelves of biscuits mysteriously emptied in the night. When the mayor called an emergency meeting to discuss the crisis she had opened the Town Hall biscuit tin to discover that someone had pinched all her gingernuts. All over town, people were putting padlocks on their lunchboxes and burglar alarms on their larders.

No one knew where the Biscuit Bandit would strike next. Bumbleford had become a CITY OF FEAR!

Woo-Woo-WOO went the patrol car. It screeched to a stop outside the supermarket, and the Bumbleford Police Force got out. There were two of them, and their names were Sergeant Gosh and PC Golightly.

'This is BRILLIANT!' shouted PC Golightly, over the jangle of the burglar alarm. 'It's so good having some proper crime to fight at last!'

'There's nothing brilliant about it, Golightly,' said Sergeant Gosh, sternly. 'It's our job as police officers to keep the people of Bumbleford and their biscuits safe, and we've failed in our duty. All these biscuit burglaries and we still have no idea who the villain or villains might be. I must admit, I'm baffled.'

Mrs Oliveira, the manager of the supermarket, came running up with the keys. 'Careful now,' said Sergeant Gosh, as she unlocked the door and they all stepped into the shop.

As the lights came on they saw the

shelves of breakfast cereal and baked beans and teabags all looking perfectly normal—but the biscuit aisle was bare!

'Crumbs!' said PC Golightly.

'Wrong, Golightly,' said Sergeant Gosh, running a finger over the empty shelves. 'The burglar or burglars didn't even leave a crumb behind. Every single biscuit—gone!'

'What, even the fig rolls? I didn't think anybody liked them.'

'Even the fig rolls,

PC Golightly. It's just as I feared . . . the Biscuit Bandit has struck again!'

'Da-da-DAHHHHHHH!' said PC Golightly, who thought some dramatic music was needed.

'But I don't understand,' said Mrs Oliveira. 'There's no sign of a break-in. The front door was locked, and the back door is locked too. How did the thief get in? How did they get out again with all my biscuits?'

'Well, PC Golightly?' asked Sergeant Gosh. PC Golightly was new to the force, and he was helping her to develop her detective skills. 'How do you think the thief got in?'

PC Golightly thought hard for a moment. 'If they didn't come in through the doors,' she said, 'they must have come in upstairs somewhere. We could be dealing with a CAT BURGLAR!'

'A cat burglar?' asked Mrs Oliveira.

'That's not an actual cat who does burgling,' said PC Golightly, helpfully.

'It's a name that we police officers use for a normal human burglar who's very clever at climbing up drainpipes and over rooftops. I bet your burglar got in that way.'

They ran upstairs to Mrs Oliveira's office. Moonlight shone in on them through a big hole in the roof. It was an unusual sort of hole, roughly the size and shape of a very plump pony. The moonlight lit up a lot of little curved marks which someone or something had left all over the carpet.

'Hoofprints!' said Mrs Oliveira.

'I don't think we're looking for a cat burglar,' said Sergeant Gosh. 'I think we're looking for a PONY BURGLAR!'

'Da-da-DAHHHHHH!'

'Please stop doing that, PC Golightly.'

TWO

ANYONE FOR SPROUT SQUASHIES?

Next morning the sun got up nice and early, and the first thing it saw was Kevin flying through the sky with Max on his back.

Max loved going out for a fly first thing in the morning. The air was so cool and fresh-smelling, and as the sun rose it lit up

the rolling green hills around Bumbleford
and the mesh of dark hedges thrown over
them like an old fishing net, with little
gaps in it that were the gateways, and
raggedy knots that were dark clumps of
trees. The River Bumble snaked all silvery
between the fields, and a few early cars
were scurrying like brightly coloured
beetles on the roads. Max felt very happy
to live in Bumbleford, and very glad to
have a best friend who could fly so that he
could see it all spread out beneath him like
this, as if the town and the countryside

around it was just a really detailed model of itself.

They flew away from the town until they could see, right on the horizon, the distant blue of hills. Those were the wild, wet hills of the Outermost West, which was where Kevin had come from. He didn't miss his old home too much, but he did like to go and check on the hills from time to time, just to make sure they were still there.

But Kevin hadn't just come out to stretch his wings and admire the view. He was on a mission. He had heard all about the dreadful biscuit burglaries which had been rocking Bumbleford, and he was really worried. If all the biscuit shops in Bumbleford had been burgled, where was he going to get his mid-morning biscuit snack from? Or his late-morning biscuit snack, or his midday biscuit snack, or his afternoon biscuit snack, or his bedtime biscuit snack? For the last few nights he had been having bad dreams where he was just about to eat a nice custard cream when it suddenly sprouted wings and flew off, too fast for Kevin to catch. So to cheer him up, Max had promised that they would fly to the nearby village of Bumblebridge and buy some biscuits from the shop there.

But when they arrived, they found the shop's window boarded up, and a sign on the door that said, NO BISCUITS. 'I'm sorry,' said the shopkeeper. 'The Biscuit Bandit broke in, the night before last, and took all my biscuits.'

'Neigh!' gasped Kevin.

'Can't you order some more in?' asked Max.

'The Bandit would just burgle me again,' said the shopkeeper. 'Keeping biscuits in my shop is just asking for trouble. I'm not ordering any more until the police have caught this fiend and put them safely behind bars.'

'Oh,' said Max sadly.

Kevin's ears and wings drooped miserably.

'You could always buy some flour, sugar, and butter and make your own biscuits,' the shopkeeper suggested.

'Custard creams?' said Kevin.

'They wouldn't be the same,' said Max. He'd made biscuits once at school and they'd turned out sort of greyish and lumpy.

'Well, I do have these,' said the shopkeeper, pointing to a stand in the corner of the shop which was piled high with packets of things that looked like biscuits, under a picture of a grinning man with a chef's hat and a trendy little beard. 'They're a new recipe from Brinsley Flan, Bumbleford's latest celebrity chef. He calls them Sprout Squashies. They're sprouts

squashed flat and baked. Brinsley says
they're like biscuits, but good for you.'

Max looked at the picture of Brinsley
Flan. The celebrity chef reminded him
of someone, but he couldn't think who.
He looked at the Sprout Squashies. They
reminded him of something too, and it was
squashed, dried sprouts. 'Are they nice?'
he asked doubtfully.

'Not really,' said the shopkeeper.
'In fact, they're absolutely disgusting.
That's why I haven't been able to sell
any. Even the Biscuit Bandit didn't take
any. But now there are no other biscuits
left I suppose people might try Sprout
Squashies instead . . .'

'No!' said Kevin. There was plenty of
grass outside to eat, and it looked a lot
nicer than squashed sprout biscuits. The
trouble was, he didn't want just to eat
grass. He wanted biscuits! He stamped his
hoof. 'I HATE the Biscuit Bandit!'

'Poor Kevin,' said Max, giving him a
hug. 'Let's hope the police will find that
rotten Bandit soon.'

They took off again, but Kevin was
still cross about the Biscuit Bandit. How

could anyone be so mean and thoughtless? It was shocking, that was what it was! He was so angry that he did a poo, even though Max's mum and dad said he mustn't poo while he was in mid-air.

There was a good reason for that rule. Fifty metres below, a boy called Zac was enjoying a walk in the fresh air when—Whooosh

SPLAT

—a big dollop of fresh, steaming pony poo landed right on his head.

'Who threw that?' shouted Zac, but there was no answer. High overhead, a plump white pony with a boy on his back went flapping away in the direction of Bumbleford.

As Kevin drew near to the block of flats where they lived, Max saw four people standing on the roof beside Kevin's nest. Even from a distance he could tell that one of the people was his mum, and another was his sister Daisy, but he couldn't work out who the other two could be. Then, as Kevin circled the rooftop and came in for a perfect four-point landing beside the pigeon coop, he saw that they were police officers.

'This is Sergeant Gosh and PC Golightly,' said Max's mum—and Max could tell from the way she said it that something was wrong. 'They want to ask Kevin a few questions.'

'Questions!' said Kevin helpfully. He had become quite well-known since he moved to Bumbleford, what with one thing and another, like rescuing all those people from the flood, and performing at Misty Twiglet's pop concert. Reporters from the Bumbleford Evening Echo and the local TV station were always asking him questions, like, 'Are unicorns overrated?' and, 'What's your favourite type of biscuit?'

'Custard creams!' said Kevin.

'Quite,' said Sergeant Gosh, very seriously. 'Now, Mr—er—Kevin, can you tell us your whereabouts on the night of 21st?'

Kevin looked blank.

'He means, where were you last night?'
explained PC Golightly.

'Here,' said Kevin. He nudged his nest
with his nose. 'Asleep. Biscuits.'

'Biscuits?' said Sergeant Gosh, suspiciously.

'LOTS of biscuits,' said Kevin. He was remembering the dream he'd had, but Sergeant Gosh took out his notebook and wrote down, *Lots of biscuits*, then gave Kevin a very stern look.

'What's all this about anyway?' said Daisy.

'It's about us investigating an extremely serious crime,' said PC Golightly. 'At around midnight last night some person or persons unknown broke into the supermarket and nicked all the biscuits!'

'Gasp!' gasped Max. 'Just like all those other burglaries!'

'Not quite,' said Sergeant Gosh. 'Because this time the burglar got careless and left some clues behind. We found hoofprints— and a hole in the roof.'

'A hole,' said PC Golightly, 'roughly the size and shape of a pony.'

'So we thought, are there any ponies in Bumbleford who can fly and have a liking for biscuits?' said Sergeant Gosh. 'It didn't take us long to narrow it down.'

'It didn't us take us long at all,' agreed PC Golightly. ''Cos there's only one, isn't there, Sarge? And it's Kevin.'

'Kevin!' said Kevin.

'It's not true!' shouted Max.

'Kevin would never steal biscuits!' yelled Daisy.

'I'm sure it's all just a misunderstanding,' said Mum.

'Really?' Sergeant Gosh reached into his pocket. 'Then perhaps THIS is a misunderstanding too?' He held out a photograph. 'We found the supermarket security camera had taken this picture of the thief as he was making his getaway.'

The photo wasn't very good. It had been taken in the night time, so it was mostly black and grey, but there was a white blur in the middle, and it was a white blur with a head and two wings and four legs and one tail.

'Kevin?' said Mum. 'Is that you?'

Kevin spread his wings in a shrug. It definitely looked like him.

'I still don't believe it,' Mum said. 'Kevin's such a well-behaved pony.'

'Are you sure about that?' asked Sergeant Gosh. He showed her a news update on his phone.

'A pony who's capable of pooing on random passers-by from a great height is capable of anything,' said Sergeant Gosh.

'So where ARE all these biscuits Kevin is supposed to have stolen?' demanded Max. He waved his hands at the mostly empty rooftop. 'There aren't any biscuits here!'

'Kevin could have eaten the evidence,' said PC Golightly. 'He certainly *looks* as if he's eaten the evidence.'

'Kevin's always been that shape!' said Daisy.

Sergeant Gosh lifted a corner of Kevin's nest. Underneath it, rustling in the morning breeze, was a huge pile of empty biscuit packets.

'I'm sorry,' said Sergeant Gosh. 'Kevin, I'm arresting you on a charge of biscuit burglary. Anything you neigh may be taken down and used in evidence against you . . .'

'What?' shouted Max. 'You're going to put him in prison? With thieves and criminals?'

'Of course not,' said PC Golightly. 'He'll be going to special Horse Prison. It's more like a kind of maximum security stable.'

'But I live here,' said Kevin, who was starting to feel a bit frightened. 'I don't want to go to Horse Prison!'

Max looked at Kevin. Could his best friend really be the dreaded Biscuit Bandit? For a moment he almost believed it. What other explanation could be there be? But as he looked into Kevin's friendly face he knew somehow that it wasn't true. Kevin loved biscuits, but not enough to steal them!

But how was Max going to make the police officers understand that? There were the hoofprints, the hole in the supermarket roof, the photo, the rustling wrappers stashed under Kevin's nest—so many clues, and they all pointed to Kevin!

'Oh Kevin!' he said. 'I don't want you to go to Horse Prison either! What are we going to do?' And his eyes filled with tears.

'Biscuits?' suggested Kevin.

'Max,' Daisy whispered in her brother's ear, 'we have to get Kevin away! We can't let him go to Horse Prison! You fly away, while I cause a distraction.' She turned to the grown-ups, pointed at the sky behind them and said in a loud voice, 'Hey! Look! Over there! It's a DISTRACTION! A really big one!'

As they all turned to look, Max took his chance. 'Fly, Kevin, FLY!' he shouted, leaping on to Kevin's back.

Kevin was still a bit confused. He was wondering if he really was a burglar, and how he could have eaten all those biscuits without remembering, because that seemed a bit of a waste, especially if they'd been nice ones. But he heard the urgency in Max's voice, so he spread his wings and took off, soaring away from the rooftop.

'Come BACK!' boomed Sergeant Gosh. 'You're under arrest!'

But Kevin and Max were already too far away to hear him. Kevin might be a bit on the roly-poly side, but he could really get a wiggle on when he wanted to. He hadn't liked being arrested at all. He flapped his little wings till they were just a blur, and zoomed off into the dazzle of the morning sun.

THREE

HIDING OUT

When they took off Max had no idea what to do or where to go. He just knew that

he couldn't let his friend be arrested. He
tried to think of somewhere in Bumbleford
where he could hide a roly-poly flying
pony. He couldn't at first, but then he
remembered Misty Twiglet. She was the
pop star who had bought a big house not
far away. There had been a bit of a mix-up
a few months before, when she had sort
of accidentally kidnapped Kevin, but that
hadn't really been her fault—it had been
the work of her villainous manager, Baz
Gumption. Max and Daisy and Kevin had
foiled Baz's schemes, and become good
friends with Misty. Max was sure she
would want to help, and that made him
feel much better. He dried his tears on
the sleeve of his jumper and told Kevin to
fly to Little Strimming, the village where

Misty lived.

Misty's house was called Gloomsbury Grange, and it looked like something out of a spooky film. It had dark walls, spiky roofs, complicated curly ironwork, and even a pair of bats. But it was mid morning when Max and Kevin got there, so the bats were in bed, and the house didn't look too spooky in the sunshine. It wouldn't have spooked Max and Kevin anyway—Misty had told them to drop in whenever they liked.

She was packing to go away when Kevin landed on the lawn. It's a busy life being an international pop sensation, and Misty was due at the National Hairstyle and Fancy Hat Awards in the big city that night (she had been nominated in two different categories: Best Original Hairstyle, and Most Unexpected Hat). Her guitarist Cardigan Faun was helping her load hatboxes into her big black car, but they stopped when Max leapt off Kevin's back and ran over to them.

'Max!' said Misty. 'And Kevin!'

'Whatever is the matter?' asked Cardigan Faun. He was an actual faun from the wild, wet hills, with horns and goat's legs and a very nice cardigan, and he could tell at a glance that Kevin was not a happy flying pony.

'We need help!' said Max.

'Help and biscuits,' said Kevin, trotting up behind him.

'The police think Kevin is the dreaded Biscuit Bandit!' Max explained.

'But that's ridiculous!' said Misty. 'Kevin's not a burglar! Is he?'

'NO!' said Kevin firmly.

'And I told them that!' said Max. 'But they won't believe me. They want to arrest Kevin and send him to Horse Prison.'

'Oh, that's bad,' said Cardigan Faun. 'I knew a unicorn who spent some time in Horse Prison. There are some really tough horses in there, and the food's horrible. It wouldn't be Kevin's type of place at all.'

PRINCESS TWINKLE HOOVES | JOEY THE MULE | STRIPES McGINTY | SHETLAND EDDIE PERKINS | POINTY STEVE

'So I was hoping he could hide here,' Max said.

'Of course,' said Misty. 'Kevin's always welcome. But don't you think the police might come and look for him here? After all, everyone knows we're good friends.'

Max hadn't thought about that, but of course Misty Twiglet was right. Far off, faint at first but growing louder, he heard the **Woo-Woo-Woo** of the Bumbleford Police Force's fastest patrol car.

'What are we going to do?' he shouted.

'Eat some biscuits?' said Kevin hopefully.

'We're going to hide Kevin, of course,' said Misty.

Not far away was the garage where she kept her cars. Cardigan Faun heaved open the doors and Max and Kevin hurried inside. The garage smelled of oil and dusty sunshine. There was an empty space where the big black car usually parked, and a small pink sports car that looked like

an expensive trainer. Misty rummaged
at the back of the garage and found a big
tarpaulin sheet. 'Kevin,' she said, 'I want
you to just stand there beside my car and
try to look like a motorbike.'

'Broom, broom,' said Kevin helpfully.

'A very QUIET motorbike,' said Max.

'Brumm, brumm,' said Kevin, very quietly. He sneezed when Max and Misty pulled the tarpaulin over him, because it was a bit dusty, but he didn't mind being covered up, not if it would stop the police taking him to Horse Prison.

'Best if they don't see you here either, Max,' said Misty. So Max went and squeezed himself into the dark corner behind Misty's sports car as the patrol car pulled up outside with a gritty grumble of gravel. Peeking over the sports car's bonnet, Max watched Misty and Cardigan Faun go outside to meet the police officers.

'Good morning, Miss Twiglet,' said Sergeant Gosh. 'We were wondering if you had time to answer a few questions?'

'Of course!' said Misty.

'Oh great!' twittered PC Golightly. 'What's it like being a famous pop star? Where do you get your ideas from? Will you follow me on Instagram? Can I have your autograph?'

'Not those sort of questions, PC Golightly,' said Sergeant Gosh.

'Oh, no Sarge—sorry Sarge . . .' The star-struck constable giggled and blushed. 'What I meant to say was, have you seen this pony?' And she held up a large picture of Kevin. 'I'm your biggest fan,' she squeaked.

Misty looked closely at the picture, and slowly shook her head. 'That's Kevin, isn't it? I haven't seen him for a couple of weeks. But I do know for a fact that he would never, ever steal biscuits!'

'We were as shocked as you are,' said Sergeant Gosh. He walked past Misty and stood in the open doorway of the garage, looking in. 'What's under that tarpaulin?'

'That's just my motorbike,' said Cardigan Faun. 'Misty lets me store it here.'

'I see. And your name is . . .'

'Cardigan Faun,' said Cardigan Faun.

'Ooh, I like your furry trousers,' said PC Golightly. 'But don't your legs get hot?'

Under his tarpaulin, Kevin tried to be as much like a quiet motorbike as possible. He remembered something Daisy had said when she was acting in the school play, how you had to become the character you were playing. He imagined his folded wings were a saddle, his hoofs were tyres, and his ears were handlebars. He imagined his tummy was full of petrol instead of biscuits. Mmm, biscuits, he thought.

'Who said that?' demanded Sergeant Gosh, looking around. 'Did someone say, "biscuits"?'

Kevin realized he had said his thought out loud. Oh no! Now Sergeant Gosh was walking into the garage!

'That was me,' said Misty quickly. 'I was just wondering if you'd like some.

Biscuits, I mean. And tea.'

'Ooh yes p—' said PC Golightly.

'Not while we're on duty, thank you, Miss,' said Sergeant Gosh firmly. He looked around the garage and then turned and went back out into the sunlight. 'We have to press on with our enquiries. We can't let that hoofed hooligan continue his one-pony crime-wave. We're becoming a laughing stock, and there's a danger of copycat crimes.'

'That's not crimes by actual cats,' explained PC Golightly. 'Sarge just means, if ordinary human people see Kevin pinching all these biscuits and getting away with it, they might decide to start nicking things themselves.'

Hidden behind the pink sports car, Max

put both hands over his mouth to stop himself from yelling, 'BUT KEVIN IS INNOCENT!'

'I still don't believe Kevin's been stealing biscuits,' said Misty Twiglet.

'Well someone has,' said Sergeant Gosh. 'And all the evidence points to your portly pony pal. You'll let us know if you do see him, won't you Miss?'

'And good luck at the big awards ceremony tonight!' said PC Golightly. 'I think your hats are all really unexpected, and your hairstyle is deffo the most original!'

And the Bumbleford Police Force got back into their car and drove away.

'Well!' said Misty, while they pulled the tarpaulin off Kevin and dusted him a bit.

'This is bad! If the police find out we've been lying to them we'll be in all sorts of trouble.'

'So what should we do?' asked Cardigan Faun.

'I don't know! I wish I didn't have to go to the big city today, but I can't get out of it—the National Hairstyle and Hat Awards are very important . . .'

'We'll have to clear Kevin's name,' said

Max. 'They can't arrest him for stealing those biscuits if we can prove it's someone else who's been stealing them all along. We just need to find out who.'

'But how?' asked Misty. 'We're not detectives.'

'Biscuits?' said Kevin, who found that being a motorbike had given him an appetite.

'Good idea,' said Misty. 'There's still an hour before I have to leave for the big city. We'll go and have some biscuits and have a good, hard think.'

But when they got to the house they had a surprise waiting for them, and it wasn't the nice sort. Misty Twiglet's larder, which was usually full of biscuits especially for when Kevin came to see her, was completely empty.

The Biscuit Bandit had struck again!

FOUR

MAX MAKES PLANS (AND BISCUITS)

Do you remember what Sergeant Gosh said about copycat crimes? Well, he was right—or half right. A crime was being plotted at that very moment, only it wasn't a copycat crime, it was more of a copy-guinea-pig crime.

Neville and Beyoncé were Bumbleford's most daring guinea pigs. That time when the whole town flooded they had floated out of the window in their hutch and ended up discovering a new country. The new country had turned out to be just the top of the park-keeper's compost heap, but it had given Neville and Beyoncé a taste for adventure, and now they were always on the lookout for fresh excitement.

They had read about the Biscuit Bandit's reign of terror in the newspapers which their owner, Ellie Fidgett, used to line their hutch. It sounded like a jolly good idea to them. They happened to know that Bumbleford Pet Shop had a lot of their favourite super tasty sunflower seeds in stock, but Ellie was saving up

her pocket money towards a new phone and couldn't afford to buy them any. If the Biscuit Bandit could get biscuits for free, Neville and Beyoncé didn't see why they shouldn't help themselves to some sunflower seeds. Anyway, they would be great at being criminals, because they both looked super cool in sunglasses, and Beyoncé was sure she would make a good getaway driver, if only they could find a guinea-pig-sized getaway car.

That morning, while Ellie was at her ballet class, the gangster guinea pigs began plotting the perfect robbery . . .

At round about that same time, Daisy's phone rang. She was on her own in the flat because Mum and Dad had gone out to look for Max and Kevin. Daisy had been expecting Max to get in touch, but she was afraid the police might be listening in, so when she answered she put on a French accent.

'Allo?' she said. 'Oo eez zees?'

'Oh, sorry,' said Max. 'I think I've got the wrong number.'

'No, eet iz mee!' said Daisy quickly, before he could hang up.

'Oo?' asked Max. 'I mean, WHO?'

'Eet eez Elvira,' said Daisy, using the name she was always trying to get everyone to call her because it sounded cooler than Daisy. 'You know, ze cool and mysterious Elvira.'

'Your voice has gone funny, Daisy,' said Max.

'Nevairr mind zat. Are you and le monsieur le Kevin all right?'

'Yes!' said Max. 'Everything's OK, and we've got a PLAN.'

'Don't tell me about it over the phone, I mean, ovairr ze phern,' said Daisy. 'I weel come to you.'

'OK!' agreed Max. 'Can you bring some biscuits? Misty's been burgled by the Biscuit Bandit!'

Daisy put away her phone and looked in her coffin-shaped money box. She had three pound coins, two buttons, and a dead moth. That should be enough for her bus fare out to Misty's place, but it wouldn't leave much for biscuits. She went to the kitchen, but the biscuit tin was empty. (It hadn't been burgled or anything—it was just that Max and Daisy and their mum and dad liked biscuits almost as much as Kevin, so they'd eaten them all.)

Luckily, as Daisy was leaving, she bumped into the downstairs neighbours, Mr and Mrs Brown.

'Do you have any biscuits I could borrow?' she asked.

'I'm sorry, Daisy dear,' said Mrs Brown, 'we're right out of biscuits.'

'It's all these burglaries,' agreed Mr
Brown. 'There's a Bumbleford-wide biscuit
shortage. It's rather exciting. How about
some cake instead?'

Daisy shook her head. Kevin wasn't that keen on cakes—he said they were a bit too cakey and not quite biscuity enough.

'Oh, I know!' said Mrs Brown. She ran back into her flat and returned holding a packet of Sprout Squashies. 'They're new,' she said. 'They're a sort of biscuit, I suppose. They're made by Brinsley Flan, Bumbleford's very own celebrity chef!'

Daisy looked at the packet. There was a cartoon on it of a friendly sprout, and a picture of Brinsley Flan saying, 'All the CRUNCH of a biscuit, all the GOODNESS of a SCRUMPTIOUS SPROUT'. The celebrity chef reminded Daisy of someone, but she could not think who.

'They're just as good as you'd expect!' said Mrs Brown.

'And they're much better for you than ordinary biscuits,' said Mr Brown.

Daisy thought Sprout Squashies looked even worse than actual sprouts, but she didn't want to offend the Browns so she said, 'Thank you!' and took the packet. She supposed the strange little greenish biscuits must be popular—she saw lots of big posters for them as she walked to the bus stop.

But then there were lots of posters of Kevin, too, and he didn't seem popular at all. The latest edition of the Bumbleford Evening News had the headline, 'Kevin the Biscuit Thief!'. Daisy stopped at a news stand to read the front page. 'Stop This Neighing Ne'r-Do-Well!' it said, and there was also an interview with Brinsley Flan saying how terrible it was when a pony turned to crime, and how he hoped the people of Bumbleford would enjoy his Sprout Squashies now all the biscuits were gone.

Daisy sighed and looked at the packet of Squashies in her hand. 'Oh well, perhaps Kevin will like them,' she thought. He liked eating grass, after all. (Just not as much as he liked eating biscuits.)

But when she reached Gloomsbury Grange it turned out Kevin didn't like Sprout Squashies one bit. Misty Twiglet had zoomed off to the big city by then, but she had said Max and Kevin could stay. They were in the kitchen with Cardigan Faun when Daisy arrived. 'Biscuits!' Kevin said happily when Daisy held one out to him.

But when he ate it his whole expression changed.

'Nasty!' he said. His tummy rumbled, and he lifted up his tail and let out a sad little fart. It was as if the ghost of the Sprout Squashie was escaping from his bum.

Max tried one too. 'Eww!' he said. 'Why would anyone want to eat one of those?'

'They were all I could find,' said Daisy. 'Apparently there's a Bumbleford-wide biscuit shortage! There are no biscuits anywhere!'

'No biscuits?' Kevin whimpered. He looked as if he was going to faint.

'Don't worry, Kevin,' said Max. 'We've got a plan, remember? We're going to find out who the REAL Biscuit Bandit is. That way we can clear your name AND make Bumbleford safe for biscuits again.'

'What is this plan?' asked Daisy.

So Max told her. It had been Kevin's idea really. Earlier on, Misty Twiglet had said, 'If only we could get the real Biscuit Bandit to show themselves,' and Max had said, 'But how?' and Kevin had said, 'Biscuits!' and Max had said, 'Kevin, you're a genius!' and Kevin had looked a bit confused and said 'Biscuits?' again, and Max had said, 'Yes!'

The plan was simple. They were going

to set a TRAP for the Biscuit Bandit. All the biscuit shops of Bumbleford had been burgled, so they would set up a new shop, and fill its windows with biscuits, and keep watch overnight, and see who arrived to burgle it. Luckily Misty had just bought a shop on Bumbleford High Street, but she hadn't moved in yet because she couldn't decide what sort of things it should sell. (Hats? Candles? Posh string? There were so many possibilities!) So the shop was empty at the moment, and Misty had lent Max and Kevin the keys.

'But where will you get all the biscuits from?' asked Daisy. 'There are no biscuits left!'

Kevin went faint again, but Max

said, 'We're going to MAKE them, of course. I made biscuits at school last term.'

'What, those lumpy grey things?' asked Daisy.

A loud bleeping noise filled the kitchen, and Max said, 'Aha! The first batch is done!'

Cardigan Faun put on oven mitts and opened the door of Misty's huge oven.

The kitchen filled with the smell of fresh, home-baked biscuits as he reached in and pulled out the tray. He put it down on the table. Max, Daisy, and Kevin stood and looked at it.

'Are you sure they're biscuits?' asked Daisy.

'I followed all the instructions,' said Max. But somehow the biscuits didn't look very biscuit-y. They had turned out sort of greyish again, except for the black bits round the edges, and they weren't really the right shape for biscuits. They weren't really the right shape for anything. 'I don't think we'll trap the Biscuit Bandit with these,' he said sadly.

'I expect they taste nice,' Daisy said, to cheer him up.

'They DON'T!' said Kevin, who had decided to test one. He spat out the bits and made a face.

Daisy's phone bleeped. She looked at the screen. 'It's a message from Mum and Dad. They're still looking for you both. They're awfully worried. They think you should come home, and Kevin should hand himself in to the police.'

'But they'll make me go to Horse Prison!' said Kevin, with a shudder.

'Maybe just for a short time, until all

this is sorted out,' said Daisy.

'It would be the sensible thing to do,' said Cardigan Faun.

'I don't like doing sensible things!' said Kevin.

'I don't see what else we can do,' said Max. 'We can't start a fake biscuit shop to trap the Bandit with if we can't bake any biscuits. It's all over. We might as well give ourselves up. Maybe they'll let me come to Horse Prison with you . . .'

Kevin sighed. He plodded outside and stood by Misty Twiglet's swimming pool, looking down at his reflection in the water. He had never felt so sad. He didn't want to go to Horse Prison, but he especially didn't want Max to have to go to Horse Prison with him. Max and Daisy were such good friends for trying to help him, but he knew that he was just getting them into trouble too. Maybe it would be better if I just went away, he thought. Maybe I'll fly back to the wild, wet hills. Surely the police won't come looking for me there . . .

But he was going to miss his friends SO MUCH. A tear dripped off the end of his nose and plopped into the swimming pool.

Just then, Max and Daisy came running out of the house with Cardigan Faun. 'Kevin!' Max shouted, 'Daisy's had an IDEA!'

Kevin looked at the air above Daisy's head to see if a lightbulb would appear there, like in cartoons, but it didn't, so he just had to imagine one.

'We CAN start a biscuit shop without biscuits!' said Daisy. 'I know exactly how we can do it!' She gave Max her phone. 'Send a message to Mum and Dad and let them know you're all right—you don't have to say where you are. Cardigan Faun, do you think Misty would mind if I used her computer?'

FIVE

BETTY'S BRILLIANT BISCUITS

That night, when darkness had fallen, Kevin flew Max and Daisy to the edge of Bumbleford and they made their way on foot into the heart of town, because they were afraid the police might be scanning the skies for low-flying ponies. They hurried through byways and back alleys to the High Street, ducking into shady doorways whenever they heard someone coming. From time to time Kevin went,

'Brumm, brummm,' in a motorbikey sort of way.

They soon found the empty shop that Misty owned—it was two doors down from Mum's hairdressing salon, but it was so late that the salon was closed, just like all the other shops. Carefully Daisy unlocked the door, and she, Max, and Kevin tiptoed and tip-hoofed inside.

The shop was busy being redecorated, so it smelled nicely of fresh paint, and there was a stepladder standing in one corner. Daisy and Max carried the ladder outside and Daisy held it while Max climbed up to stick a new sign above the shop window. Max and Daisy had made this sign themselves, and they both thought it had turned out very well.

As you can see, there were pictures of biscuits all around the words, and also quite a lot of hoofprints where Kevin had

accidentally walked through the wet paint,
but they hoped no one would notice those.

When the sign was in
place, and as straight as
they could get it, they
went back inside the
shop and started filling
the window with the things they
had brought with them in Max's rucksack.
There were the sad little biscuits he had
baked, which didn't look so bad any more
because Daisy had covered them with
chocolate and hundreds-and-thousands.
There were also lots of boxes with
bright labels covered
in pictures of
biscuits. The
boxes didn't

really have biscuits in—they were just empty shoeboxes rescued from Misty's recycling bin which Daisy had covered in bright biscuit pictures she had printed off from the internet. But nobody looking in through the window would know that. They would think these were family-size boxes of custard creams, party rings, and those ones with the cows on. And hopefully, if the person looking in was the Biscuit Bandit, they would break in and steal them and fall right into Max and Kevin's Cunning Trap . . .

So Max and Daisy arranged the biscuit boxes as neatly as they could, and turned a light on in the window, and crept into a shadowy alcove at the back of the shop where they sat down next to Kevin and waited to be burgled.

Laying a trap for a fiendish biscuit burglar turned out to be more boring than they'd expected. There wasn't a lot of room in the shadowy alcove. Also, it was a long time since lunch, and Kevin's tummy was starting to rumble. Even the biscuits Max had baked were starting to smell quite nice to him. 'Biscuit?' he suggested.

'You can't eat those, Kevin,' said Daisy. 'They're the bait!'

'Shhh!' said Max. 'Listen!'

They all listened, but they didn't hear a Biscuit Bandit—they heard the **Woo-Woo-Woo** of the police patrol car.

'Perhaps someone saw us!' said Daisy. 'Perhaps the police have worked out Kevin's here, and they're coming to arrest him!'

'Brumm!' said Kevin, trying to

~88~

look like a motorbike again.

The **Woo-Woo-Woo** got louder, and louder, and louder . . . and then quieter again, as the patrol car went speeding past. Sergeant Gosh and PC Golightly weren't interested in the new biscuit shop. They were on their way to a different crime scene.

'Phew!' said Max.

After that it was quiet again for a bit, except for the soft rumbly sounds of Kevin's tum.

'Just one biscuit?' he asked politely.

'No,' said Max. 'We mustn't disturb the window display.'

'I wish he'd hurry up,' grumbled Kevin.

Just then from somewhere upstairs, there came a tinkle of breaking glass and a

loud **BOMP.**

'Something landed on the roof!'
whispered Max.

'Something's coming down the stairs!'
hissed Daisy.

'Shhhhh!' said everybody, and they
clung together and waited for their first
glimpse of the Biscuit Bandit.

Down the stairs came a shadowy shape.
A roly-poly sort of shape, with four legs,
and two wings . . . For a horrible moment
Max thought, 'It's all TRUE, Kevin
really IS the Biscuit Bandit!' But when he
checked, Kevin was still right beside him,
looking just as confused as everybody else.

It didn't make sense. How could there
be TWO Kevins?

HOW???

Meanwhile, Sergeant Gosh and PC Golightly were investigating a different robbery. This one had taken place in the Bumbleford Toy and Games Centre. The owner, Mr Midgeley, had just been locking up for the night when someone had burst in and driven off in one of the remote control cars from his window display. 'It was a little hairy person,' said Mr Midgeley, who was a bit short-sighted. 'Very cool sunglasses though.'

'Could it be the Biscuit Bandit?' asked PC Golightly. 'Perhaps now he's stolen all the biscuits he's moved on to stealing cars. He's starting with really little ones, for practice.'

'Hmmm,' said Sergeant Gosh. 'I don't think this is the work of the Biscuit Bandit. I think we have another criminal in town . . .'

He was right! Beyoncé the guinea pig drove her new getaway car into an alley behind the bus station where Neville was waiting with a can of quick-drying bright red spray paint. They resprayed the car so no one would recognize it, and set off in the direction of the pet shop, where

all those lovely sunflower seeds sat, just
waiting to be burgled.

They had to drive right past the Toy
and Games centre on their way. PC
Golightly looked up from her notebook
and saw the little car go trundling by. 'Er,
Mr Midgeley,' she said, 'what colour was
the stolen vehicle?'

'Blue,' said Mr Midgeley.

'Not red?'

'No, definitely blue.'

'Oh,' said PC Golightly, and went back to writing down the details of the crime.

υυυ

In their pretend biscuit shop Kevin, Max, and Daisy watched in amazement as the other Kevin went creeping towards the display of biscuit boxes in the window.

'This is Very Confusing,' whispered Kevin.

But as the other Kevin stepped into the light of the window they started to see that there was something odd about him. Instead of a nice glossy coat like Kevin's, this pony looked all grubby and tufty, like an old bath mat that's been left out in the rain. His wings hung limply from his back as if they'd been cut out of cardboard and covered with blobs of cotton wool by someone who didn't have quite enough glue, or quite enough cotton wool. Instead of walking or trotting, he sort of shambled along, with strange lumps coming and going under his skin. And what was that shiny line around his middle? It looked like a zipper!

'He's just a pantomime horse!' whispered Max.

The fake pony heard him. His head swung towards the alcove where the friends were hiding. **EEP!** he said.

That wasn't the sort of noise a pony usually made. It sounded more like . . .

'Sea Monkeys!' said Kevin.

He was right.

The Sea Monkeys had first arrived in Bumbleford at the same time as Kevin, when that storm sent loads of water gushing down the river Bumble to flood the whole town. They were mischievous, noisy, bad-mannered creatures who had caused no end of trouble. When the flood waters drained away the Sea Monkeys had vanished, driving off in Mr and Mrs Brown's old camper van. Max had sometimes wondered where they were and what they were doing. And now he knew! They were all crammed inside a pantomime horse costume with unconvincing wings, and they were busy burgling his pretend biscuit shop!

The Sea Monkeys were so surprised to see Max, Kevin, and Daisy waiting there that they all jumped, and the zipper around the suit's middle burst open, spilling the naughty little creatures all over the floor.

They scrambled back up onto each other's shoulders, trying to drag the pony suit back together around them. '**EEEP! EEP! EEEP!**' they squeaked.

'Now cut that out,' said Daisy. 'We've caught you fair and square. Sit still and keep quiet while I phone the police.'

But Sea Monkeys aren't much good at sitting still or keeping quiet, and this lot didn't see why they should hang around until the police arrived. Stumbling along in their sagging pony suit, they blundered back up the stairs.

'Stop them!' shouted Max. 'They're getting away!'

Kevin neighed and went after the monkeys, up the stairs and through the empty rooms above the shop. Broken glass glittered under the window where the fake pony had smashed its way in. The monkeys paused under it. There was no way they could fly out using their silly cardboard pony wings.

'Stop!' Kevin whinnied sternly. 'You're in big trouble! You're going to Horse Prison! Or Monkey Prison.'

'**EEEP! EEP! EEEP!**' giggled the monkeys. One of them pulled something out from inside the pony suit. It was a king-size packet of Sprout Squashies. The monkeys each quickly ate one of the sprouty snacks, pulling horrible faces at the taste. '**BLEUGH! EWW! PLEUGH!**' they said. Then their tummies started to rumble.

'Quickly!' shouted Kevin, who could hear his friends running up the stairs

behind him. Max and Daisy burst into the room. 'Catch them!' Kevin whinnied.

But before any of them could do anything, those Sprout Squashies took effect. The Sea Monkeys all farted in unison—**FUURP BLAAAT BRRRRUUUB SQUEEB!**—and the fake pony blasted off, shot through the broken skylight, and vanished into the midnight sky.

'They escaped!' said Daisy, flapping her hand in front of her nose to clear away the sprouty stench. She kicked a Sprout Squashie so hard that it zoomed across the floor like a hockey puck and made a dent in the skirting board.

Max felt downhearted too. Their clever plan to trap the Biscuit Bandit had failed, and all they were left with was a broken window and a peculiar smell. 'It doesn't make sense,' he complained. 'Why would a load of monkeys dress themselves up as Kevin and go around stealing biscuits?'

'Not just any monkeys,' said Daisy. 'Sea Monkeys! They're the naughtiest sort of monkeys!'

'But surely they aren't brainy enough to plan a whole series of burglaries, or patient enough to come up with a convincing pony costume,' said Max.

'They must be working for someone else!' said Kevin.

'You mean a criminal mastermind is paying them with bananas or something to steal biscuits from all Bumbleford's shops?' asked Daisy.

'What's a crim . . . crimninal mastermind?' asked Kevin.

'Someone who's made those monkeys dress up as you and hide biscuit wrappers under your nest so that you get the blame!' said Max.

'But why would a crimninal mastermind want to do that?' asked Kevin, feeling a bit hurt.

'I don't know,' said Max, scrambling up

onto Kevin's back. 'But I know how to find out!
FOLLOW THAT PANTOMIME PONY!'

Daisy climbed onto Kevin's back too, and
the little pony took off, flying up through the
hole the monkeys had made and following
the fading trail of sprout-farts across the
rooftops of the sleeping town.

SIX

BUMBLEFORD'S MOST
EXCITING NIGHT EVER

Mr and Mrs Perkins, the owners of
Bumbleford Pet Shop, had been very
worried by all the recent burglaries. They
didn't sell biscuits in their shop, but they
did sell dog biscuits. Perhaps when the
Biscuit Bandit had stolen all the people
biscuits he would start stealing dog
biscuits too! They had put extra locks on
their doors and windows, and Mr Perkins

had installed a brand new burglar alarm system, but they were still uneasy.

That night, in their flat above the shop, Mrs Perkins woke Mr Perkins up.

'I heard a noise!' she said. 'From downstairs!'

'It's probably just an over-excited gerbil,' said Mr Perkins sleepily. 'Very excitable animals, gerbils.'

'It wasn't a gerbil sort of noise,' said Mrs Perkins. 'It was more of a burglar sort of noise.'

So Mr Perkins got grumpily out of bed and made his way downstairs. The pet shop was all in darkness, and silent except for the small snores coming from the hutches and cages where the pets lived. Even the gerbils were asleep. Across the floor the laser beams of the brand new burglar alarm drew a glowing grid. Any burglar who walked through one of those beams would set off the alarm. Careful not to break the beams himself, Mr Perkins had a good look around, checked that the door was locked, then stomped off back to bed.

'It's as safe as the Bank of England down there,' he told Mrs Perkins.

But as soon as he had gone, an air vent in the ceiling above the sunflower seed display flipped open. Neville lowered

himself down
over the display
on a complicated
arrangement of strings
and pulleys. Dangling
just above the shelves,
the daring guinea pig
began loading packets
of sunflower seeds into
his backpack.

SUN
FLOWER
SEEDS

BAAAARP! FOOP! CHUFF! RuuUuuUuULrmp! SQUEEEEB! went the sprout-powered pantomime pony, rocketing its way between the chimney pots. The Sea Monkeys' way of flying was fast, but their steering wasn't very good—they kept bumping into rooftops and dinging off satellite dishes. Kevin flew after them, his small wings going **FLIP FLAP FLIP FLAP** so fast that they were just a blur.

But those monkeys had a head start, and Kevin was slowed down a bit by having to carry Max and Daisy. It was all he could do to keep the fake pony in sight.

'HA HA HA! EEP!' jeered the Sea Monkeys, landing with a crash on a shop roof and rocketing off again in a cloud of sprout-fumes and broken slates. 'You can't catch us!'

'Keep going, Kevin!' Max told his friend. 'They're heading for the edge of town . . .'

The roof the monkeys had just hit
belonged to Bumbleford Pet Shop.
'Burglars!' screamed Mrs Perkins, woken
by the loud **CRASH** from above.
Mr Perkins got out of bed again and
ran to the window, but by the time he
opened it and stuck his head out there was
nothing to be seen. Strange noises echoed
across the town—**TRRRUMP!** and **FLIP FLAP FLIP
FLAP**—and the night air had an odd
odour. Mr Perkins sniffed suspiciously.
'Smells like sprouts . . .' he said.

The Perkinses weren't the only
ones who had been startled by the Sea
Monkeys' collision with their roof. The
sound went echoing down into the shop,
where Neville was carefully heaving his

backpack full of ill-gotten sunflower seeds up into the air vent. The distant CRASH made him jump and he almost dropped the backpack! He caught it just in time, but one single sunflower seed squeezed out . . .

Neville watched in horror as the seed went tumbling towards the floor—

where it bounced once—

—twice—

—and went straight through one of the blue beams which triggered the burglar alarm!

DANGANANGANANGA

'Burglars!' shouted Mr Perkins, bursting into the shop. He was carrying an air gun loaded with tiny tranquilizer darts which he kept in case the gerbils got really excited. He pointed it at different parts of the shop, but there was no sign of the burglar. Then, almost lost in the racket that the new alarm was making, he heard little footsteps go scurrying along the air duct above his head.

'Gotcha!' said Mr Perkins.

Outside the toy shop, Sergeant Gosh and PC Golightly were just climbing into their patrol car when they heard the burglar alarm. They drove quickly up the High Street towards the pet shop. The shop was completely covered in blue and red flashing lights which spelled out the words

HELP! POLICE! As they pulled up outside, the door burst open and Mr Perkins came rushing out, still clutching his tranquillizer gun. 'Stop them!' he shouted.

'Sarge, look!' squeaked PC Golightly, pointing down the alley beside the pet shop.

An air vent on the side of the building was hanging open. A hairy little shape dropped down from it. A moment later two tiny headlights came on in the shadows among the dustbins, and a small car came zooming out of the alley. It tipped up on two wheels as Beyoncé steered it past the startled police officers and took off down the High Street.

'Get in the car, Golightly!' ordered Sergeant Gosh.

'Coo, Sarge, are we going to have

a real live car chase?' said PC Golightly, as she jumped in and did up her seat belt. (She was really enjoying herself. This was EXACTLY the type of thing she'd been hoping for when she joined the police force.)

Sergeant Gosh didn't bother to say, 'Yes!'. He just swung the patrol car around and set off after the escaping guinea pigs.

'Phyllis!' shouted Mr Perkins, not wanting to miss a second of what was turning into Bumbleford's most exciting night ever.

'Fetch our bicycle!'

SEVEN
THE SHOUTY SPROUT

Max and Daisy's mum and dad were very laid-back sort of parents. They didn't mind their children going off into town on their own, or zooming around the sky on a flying pony. But even they had to draw a line somewhere, and the thought of Max and Daisy staying out all night and maybe getting in trouble with the police made them feel that they should *Do* Something.

The trouble was, what could they do?

When Mum had a message from Daisy
saying she and Max were safe and not to
worry she had immediately texted back
to say, 'Come home now! I'm sure we can
work everything out, smiley face.' (Mum's
phone didn't do emojis so she had to write
them out the long way in words.) After
half an hour, when there was no answer,
she had sent another text to say, 'Daisy,
come home NOW and bring Max and
Kevin with you! Cross face, cross face,
cross face!'.

After another half hour she said to Dad, 'I bet they've gone to Misty's place at Little Strimming.' So they got into Dad's van and set off to look for the runaways.

If they had happened to look up as they were driving away from their block of flats they would have seen Kevin swoosh overhead with Max and Daisy clinging to his back. But they didn't, and Max, Kevin and Daisy didn't notice the van go by beneath them either—they had other things on their minds. Flapping furiously, Kevin followed the Sea Monkeys over the new housing estate, across the canal, over the park and the children's playground. Beyond the playground was a high wall, and beyond the wall was a big factory. It had once been the Bumbleford Biscuit Factory, but it had closed down years ago. Now it was under new ownership: **FLANTASTIC SNACKS—HOME OF THE SPROUT SQUASHIE** read the big sign outside it, and there was a picture of that cartoon sprout saying, 'Let's Shout About Sprouts!'

The fake flying pony landed with a splat and a lot of eeping in the car park outside the factory, and waddled in through the big front door. Kevin touched down gracefully on the factory's flat roof.

EEP!

'But why would they come here?' asked Daisy.

'Maybe they're out of fuel and need more Sprout Squashies,' said Max.

'Ooh, look, a big window,' said Kevin. Somebody had turned a light on inside the factory and it was shining up through a large glass skylight in the roof nearby. 'A big lying down sort of window,' he said.

They all went over and peered down through the glass, into the factory. They could see the conveyor belts, and cookie-cutters, and other machinery that made Sprout Squashies, gleaming below them like the upperworks of a sunken ship at the bottom of a lake. They could see the Sea Monkeys in their pantomime pony costume. And they could see someone else standing in the shadows.

'That must be the criminal mastermind!' said Daisy. 'He must have broken into the factory! The Sea Monkeys have come here to meet him . . .'

Just then the figure below them stepped out of the shadows into the light.

'Gasp!' whinnied Kevin. 'The crimninal misterman is a GIANT SPROUT!'

'Don't be silly,' Max said. 'That's too weird even for Bumbleford. It's just a giant sprout *costume*. I expect he's wearing that so that the Sea Monkeys don't know who they're really working for and can't go telling everyone. Sea Monkeys are probably rubbish at keeping secrets.'

Carefully, Max crept out onto the skylight. It wasn't made of glass—it was some sort of thick, clear plastic. If he pressed his ear to it, he could dimly hear the conversation going on down below him.

'What do you mean, you couldn't get the biscuits?' the sprout was shouting. 'I told you to burgle that new biscuit shop, how dare you come back empty-handed?'

'Max, what's happening?' hissed Daisy.

'The Sea Monkeys are getting a proper telling off,' said Max.

'Good!' said Daisy, and she came creeping out onto the skylight beside him and put her ear to the plastic too.

'You can get right back to that biscuit shop and finish the job properly or it'll be no bananas for you!' the sprout yelled.

'That is a very shouty sprout,' said Daisy.

Kevin had never heard a sprout shout before, so he walked onto the skylight too, and put one of his ears against the plastic.

'I don't want to see a single biscuit on sale anywhere in the Greater Bumbleford area tomorrow morning!' raged the angry sprout.

'What a mean sprout!'
Max started to say. Then he stopped.
There was an odd creaking noise
going on. It had been going on for
a little while, and it was starting
to worry him a bit. 'How many
people and ponies do you think
a skylight like this is designed
to hold?' he asked Daisy.

Daisy did a quick
calculation. 'At a guess,
I'd say . . . none?'

'Aaaaargh!' they all
said, as the plastic gave
way beneath them and
they plummeted into
the factory.

EIGHT

KEVIN AND THE SQUASHIE FACTORY

Things were still going excitingly in Bumbleford town centre. The guinea-pig-getaway car wasn't as fast as Sergeant Gosh and PC Golightly's patrol car, but it could go through narrow spaces where the patrol car wouldn't fit, and Beyoncé was just as good at driving as she'd imagined. With the blue lights of the police car lighting up the night behind them, she and Neville zoomed along pavements, smashed through a pile of tiny boxes in the alleyway behind the model railway shop, and narrowly avoided collisions with bouncing satsumas as the patrol car knocked over Bumbleford's All-Night Fruit Stall.

Meanwhile, Max and Daisy's mum and dad were still out looking for their children. They had driven all the way to Little Strimming, but there had been no answer when they rang the bell on Misty Twiglet's gates. They were just driving back into Bumbleford when suddenly a teeny-tiny car full of guinea pigs shot out of a turning just ahead of them, closely followed by a bigger car full of police officers. Dad stopped his van just in time, and he and Mum sat watching as the two cars screeched over Bumbleford Bridge and roared away into the darkness. Then a tandem bicycle came wobbling out of the turning and followed them, with Mrs Perkins from the toyshop pedalling furiously in front, and Mr Perkins sitting behind her with an air gun.

'Well,' said Mum, 'that's something you don't see every day.'

Dad said, 'I wonder if it's got something to do with . . .'

'Kevin!' they both said, and Dad revved the van's engine and sped off in pursuit.

Down under the bridge a very cross and very sleepy duck started writing another letter to the council.

‍ ‍ ‍ ‍ ‍ ‍ ‍ 🐴🐴🐴

'**AAARGH!**' went Max and Daisy, plunging through the skylight into the Sprout Squashies factory.

'**AAAARGH!**' whinnied Kevin, plunging with them (because in all the excitement he had forgotten he could fly).

'**AAAAARGH!**' shouted the shouty sprout (because he had been standing right underneath the skylight).

'**EEEEEEP!**' screamed the Sea Monkeys, who thought it was all brilliant fun.

Max, Kevin, and Daisy landed right on top of the sprout. The big soft costume cushioned their fall, but it burst under Kevin's weight, revealing the man inside it. A man with a badly dented chef's hat and a trendy little beard . . .

'It's Brinsley Flan!' gasped Daisy. 'The Biscuit Bandit is none other than Bumbleford's own celebrity chef!'

'His beard's gone funny,' neighed Kevin.

Sure enough, Brinsley Flan's beard and curly moustache were wobbling, knocked askew when Kevin squashed him. Suddenly, Max knew why the celebrity chef had looked so familiar. He reached up and pulled the fake moustache off, to reveal—a real moustache underneath! It was the moustache of their old enemy, Baz Gumption.

'Gasp!' gasped Daisy.
'So Brinsley Flan was really Baz Gumption in disguise all along!'

'Why?' asked Kevin, who was getting confused.

'Because I couldn't get any work as a pop star's manager after you lot made Misty Twiglet fire me, that's why,' growled Baz Gumption, tearing his false beard off and throwing it away. (The beard landed on a nearby Sea Monkey.)

EEP!

'So I changed my name and set up in the celebrity chef business instead.'

'And the biscuit burglary business!' said Daisy.

'You're under arrest!' neighed Kevin sternly.

Baz Gumption laughed. 'You can't arrest me! You're not a police horse, you're just a fat flying pony.'

'But we know what you've been up to!' said Daisy.

'You've been stealing all the biscuits!' said Max. 'You tried to make it look as if Kevin was doing it, but it was you all along! You're the Biscuit Bandit!'

'Yes!' said Baz. 'I thought I could easily make my fortune baking cheap sprouts into expensive snacks, but it turns out nobody likes them—who could have seen that coming? So I decided the only way to sell them was by making sure there were no other biscuits in the shops at all— then people would HAVE to eat Sprout Squashies! The only problem was—how could I burgle ALL the biscuit shops? Then by pure luck I met the Sea Monkeys, and they agreed to work for me in exchange for bananas.'

'BANANAS!' cheered the Sea Monkeys.

'They're so stupid I don't even have to give them real bananas,' Baz whispered. 'I just paint courgettes yellow, it's much cheaper. And to throw the police off the scent I thought I'd pin the blame on your flying pony friend. But of course you'll never be able to prove any of this. I'll just call the police and tell them you broke into my factory. You'll be in a stack of trouble, and your stupid pony will be off to Horse Prison!'

'But we CAN prove it, Baz Gumption!' said Daisy. She pulled out her mobile phone. 'I just recorded everything you said!'

Baz's smug smile faded. 'Monkeys!' he shouted. 'Seize them! Grab that phone!'

If there's one thing Sea Monkeys like even more than courgettes painted yellow, it's seizing people and grabbing things. With a great chorus of *eeps* all the monkeys dived for Max and Daisy. But Kevin wasn't having that. His friends had worked hard to help him, and now it was his turn to help them. 'Bad monkeys!' he shouted, and plonked himself in front of the first wave of Sea Monkeys like a plump white barrier. Sea Monkeys bounced off him, and one of them landed on the big red button that started the Sprout Squashie machines working. The noise of the conveyor belt added to the confusion as the Sea Monkeys attacked again. Baz

Gumption cheered them on, but Max and Daisy were ready for them this time. A big vat of Sprout Squashie mix was gurgling and burbling up above them, and Squashie-sized dollops of sprout mix were being plooped onto the conveyor belt. Max and Daisy started scooping up the dollops and throwing them like green snowballs in the monkeys' faces. **SPLAT! SPLODGE! SPLUNGE! EEP!** screeched the monkeys. As they staggered blindly about with their faces covered in green gloop, Kevin took hold of their tails in his mouth, and flew up with them one by one to drop into the vat of Squashie mix. The machinery got confused and started squirting bigger and bigger dollops down onto the conveyor belt.

'Stop this nonsense!' screamed Baz Gumption. 'Get those monkeys out of my Squashie mix! Nobody will want to eat it if they've been in it!'

'Nobody wants to eat it anyway!' Max started to say, but while he was saying it three especially cheeky monkeys picked him up and threw him onto the conveyor belt, just as the machine dolloped its biggest dollop yet. 'Eurgh!' said Max as the sticky mixture dropped on him.

EEP!

EEP!

EEP!

He felt a bit like Zac when he got hit by pony poo back on page 28, except Sprout Squashie mix smelled worse, and there was a LOT more of it. It covered Max completely, and it was so claggy that he couldn't move, except to wipe some of it off his face. He wished he hadn't, because once his eyes weren't full of Squashie mix any more he could see where the conveyor belt was carrying him.

A few metres ahead, the dollops of mixture were being squashed flat by a huge mechanical hammer, and then baked by a giant blowtorch!

'Help!' screamed Daisy, seeing what was about to happen. 'Max is going to get turned into Sprout Squashies!'

'EEP!' squeaked the Sea Monkeys, who

weren't really *that* naughty and were
horrified at what they'd done.

'Get off that conveyor belt!'
ordered Baz Gumption. 'My Squashies are
meant to be suitable for vegetarians!'

But Max couldn't get off—the Squashie
mix was as thick and sticky as quicksand.

So Kevin came to the rescue. From high
up above he saw what was happening, and
swooped down like a majestic eagle, only
rounder and whiter, and not actually much
like an eagle at all. Bravely sticking his nose
into the dollop of Squashie mix, he took
a firm hold of the back of Max's trousers
and lifted him clear just as the dollop was
squashed flat by the mechanical hammer.

Daisy cheered. Even the remaining Sea
Monkeys cheered, but Kevin took hold

of their tails and flew them up to drop them in the big vat along with the others, just to be safe—he'd had quite enough Sea Monkey mischief for one night. Then he glided down to land beside Max, while Daisy ran to turn off the conveyor belt.

As the noise of the machinery faded,

EEP!

FTHTHHHHHH

they heard a new sound. It was faint at first, but growing louder, and it was the **WOO-WOO-WOO** of the Bumbleford Police Force's fastest patrol car.

'The police are on their way!' said Daisy. 'Just wait till I play them my recording of you spilling the beans!'

'Beans?' said Kevin, a bit confused, because he hadn't seen any beans, only sprouts.

But Baz Gumption wasn't confused; he knew he was in Big Trouble. He turned and ran. 'You can't catch me!' he shouted.

NINE

THE FAST AND THE FURRY

Outside, Bumbleford's first high-speed car chase was still going well. It was a really good one, and PC Golightly was enjoying it a lot. 'Wheeee!' she said. 'Faster, Sarge! We've nearly got them!'

The guinea pig getaway car was bathed in light as the patrol car roared up close behind it. But suddenly Beyoncé did a handbrake turn, shot off the road and into the park, where the patrol car couldn't follow. The guinea pigs squeaked with laughter as they zoomed past the rose garden and under a gate into the children's play area. Swings and slides loomed up ahead. Beyond them was a high wall, and beyond the wall were the dark sheds and outbuildings of the Flantastic Snacks Factory, where the cops would never be able to catch two guinea pigs.

But how to get over that wall?

Beyoncé patted Neville's paw. Then she put her foot down, and aimed the car towards the base of the slide. It raced up the long silver slope of the slide and shot off the top. They were airborne!

Actually, they were a bit more airborne than Beyoncé had planned.

They flew right over the wall and kept

on flying.

'Aaaaaaaaaaaaaaargh!' they screamed.

'Aaaaaaaaaaaaaaargh!' screamed Baz Gumption, as he burst out through the front door of his factory just in time to see a tiny car and two horrified guinea pigs hurtling through the air towards him.

With a loud **DOOF** the car hit him right on the nose. 'Ow!' he said, and toppled backwards, stunned.

Kevin, Max, and Daisy came running out of the factory at the same moment as the police patrol car came screeching into

the car park.

The police officers leapt out. 'That was brilliant!' giggled PC Golightly. 'Can we do it again?'

Sergeant Gosh had some questions, too. 'What's been happening here?' he asked. 'And why are there sunflower seeds everywhere?'

Daisy pointed. 'Brinsley Flan is really Baz Gumption and both of them are the dreaded Biscuit Bandit!'

'And if it hadn't been for that interfering pony I'd have gotten clean away with it!' grumbled Baz, getting up.

'Go on,' said Max, 'arrest him!'

Sergeant Gosh looked serious. 'If I'm going to arrest him, I'll need some proof . . .'

'Daisy has proof!' said Max. 'She

recorded it on her phone while Baz was spilling the beans!'

'WHAT beans?' asked Kevin.

'No, I didn't,' said Daisy. 'That was just a fib. I wanted him to *think* we had proof. My phone actually ran out of charge ages ago.'

'In that case,' said Baz Gumption, brightening up, 'It's just these kids' word against mine! I'm innocent! It's them and Kevin who are the real Biscuit Bandits! Officers, arrest that flying pony!'

Everyone looked at Kevin, but Kevin was gone. All that talk of beans had made him feel hungry, so he had wandered off, following an interesting scent. The scent led to the door of a big shed in the corner of the car park. He butted his nose against the door.

'Look! I think he's trying to tell us something!' said PC Golightly.

Kevin was. 'Biscuits!' he said.

Max ran to join him, and together they heaved the big, heavy door open. Lights came on inside the shed. Kevin gasped, and so did everyone else.

The shed was stacked to the rafters with packets and packets of biscuits.

'These must be the ones that were stolen from all the shops in Bumbleford!'

said PC Golightly.

'Baz Gumption, I'm arresting you in the name of the law,' said Sergeant Gosh.

Before anyone could say anything else a builder's van came screeching into the car park. Mum and Dad jumped out and came running over to hug Max and Daisy and Kevin. While everyone was busy, Baz Gumption saw one last chance and made a run for it. 'STOP THAT CHEF!' bellowed Sergeant Gosh, spotting him as he sprinted out of the gate.

But the only person who could have caught up with him by then was Kevin, and Kevin was a bit distracted.

Luckily, just at that moment, a tandem came clattering down the road to the factory. 'Stop him! He's the Biscuit Bandit!' Max and Daisy shouted at the tops of their voices. The tandem had already passed Baz Gumption, but Mr Perkins swung round in his saddle and shot a gerbil tranquilizer dart at him. It hit Baz on the bottom. 'Ow!' he yelled, but since he was quite a lot bigger than a gerbil, it didn't slow him down much. So Mr Perkins fired another dart and then another, and at last Baz keeled over into a hedge and started snoring.

'Kevin,' said Sergeant Gosh, when the snoozing biscuit thief had been handcuffed and hoisted into the back of the patrol car, 'I owe you an apology. You've done excellent work. I'm sorry we ever believed you were to blame for the burglaries.'

'Biscuits?' said Kevin hopefully, feeling he deserved a reward.

The sergeant looked at the huge stack of stolen biscuits stashed in Baz Gumption's shed. A lot of them were already past their sell-by date. 'I'm sure the shopkeepers of Bumbleford wouldn't mind if you were to have a custard cream,' he said. 'Or even two.'

'Biscuits!' said Kevin happily.

TEN

TIDYING UP

After that Max, Kevin, and Daisy told the whole story to PC Gosh and Sergeant Golightly, and Mr and Mrs Perkins told theirs to some reporters from the local TV station who had just turned up. Mum and Dad went into the factory and used a ladder from Dad's van to climb up and peer into the Squashie mix vat. By that time the mix had started to harden into one huge Sprout Squashie, with bored Sea Monkeys stuck

in it like the chocolate chips in a chocolate chip cookie. Sergeant Gosh arranged for a helicopter to hoist it up through the broken skylight and fly it down to the coast at Farsight Cove. The giant Squashie was dropped far out at sea, where it dissolved, turning the waves an odd shade of green for a while. The Sea Monkeys swam off without even saying thank you, and that was the last anyone saw of them for a bit.

Misty Twiglet didn't win the Most Unexpected Hat award—in a surprise decision the judges awarded that trophy to a last-minute entry, a boy named Zac wearing a remarkable creation called "Poo de la Pony".

Misty didn't mind though, because she
still won Best Original Hairstyle. When
she came back to Bumbleford she was
so impressed by what Max and Daisy
had done that she decided to keep the

BETTY'S BRILLIANT BISCUITS

sign on her new shop and turn it into a
biscuit café. And she was so impressed by
what Kevin had done that she made him the
new café's Official Biscuit Taster and he got
to taste all the different types of biscuits
to see if they were nice. (Kevin wasn't very
good at it, because he thought ALL biscuits

were nice, but

nobody minded.)

Neville and Beyoncé had sneaked away
unnoticed after they crashed their getaway
car. They found their way back to Ellie
Fidgett's house, climbed back into their
hutch, and sat there innocently pretending
to be asleep when she came to say hello to
them next morning. But they had lost all
the sunflower seeds they stole, and it had
rained quite hard on them during the long
walk home, so they had definitely learned
that Crime Does Not Pay. In fact they felt
quite sorry for themselves for a couple of
hours and vowed that never again would

they leave their nice, cosy hutch. Then
they cheered up, and started planning
their next adventure.

Baz Gumption had learned that crime
doesn't pay too. He was sent to prison for
six months, which doesn't sound like very
long after all the trouble he'd caused. But
because of a typing error he got sent to
Horse Prison by mistake, and six months in
Horse Prison is long enough for anyone—
some of those horses are really tough, and
there was nothing to eat but hay.

A few days later, when everything was back to normal, or at least as normal as things ever got in Bumbleford, Max and Daisy were sitting on the edge of Kevin's nest after school, watching him eat his late-afternoon biscuit snack. It was a lovely warm Friday afternoon, the sunshine lay like honey on the roofs of Bumbleford, and they could see all the way to the wild, wet hills of the Outermost West.

'So what have you learned from this latest adventure, Kevin?' asked Daisy.

Kevin finished his biscuit and had a think. 'Nothing,' he said happily.

'Well, I've learned something,' said Max. 'I've learned that Kevin is my best friend ever.'